RHYME · TIME · READERS

D0232669

A Note to Parents

Rhyme, Repetition, and Reading are 3 R's that make learning fun for your child. **Rhyme Time Readers** will introduce your child to the sounds of language, providing the foundation for reading success.

Rhyme

Children learn to listen and to speak before they learn to read. When you read this book, you are helping your child connect spoken language to written language. This increased awareness of sound helps your child with phonics and other important reading skills. While reading this book, encourage your child to identify the rhyming words on each page.

Repetition

Rhyme Time Readers have stories that your child will ask you to read over and over again. The words will become memorable due to frequent readings. To keep it fresh, take turns reading and encourage your child to chime in on the rhyming words.

Reading

Someday your child will be reading this book to you, as learning sounds leads to reading words and finally to reading stories like this one. I hope this book makes reading together a special experience.

Have fun and take the time to let your child read and rhyme.

Francie Alexander

—Chief Education Officer,
Scholastic's Learning Ventures

To Erin, E.E.
—R.K.

For Clementine and Toby,
my two little butterflies
—R.E.

ISBN-13: 978-0-545-08359-1
ISBN-10: 0-545-08359-1

Text copyright © 2009 by Robin Koontz
Illustrations copyright © 2009 by Rebecca Elliott

12 11 10 9 8 7 6 5 4 3 2   9 10 11 12 13 14/0

Printed in the U.S.A.
First printing, March 2009

RHYME • TIME • READERS

Butterfly Spring

by Robin Koontz
Illustrated by Rebecca Elliott

SCHOLASTIC INC.

New York   Toronto   London   Auckland   Sydney
Mexico City   New Delhi   Hong Kong   Buenos Aires

Early one morning
I wake up and I shout:
"I'm trapped in a cocoon—
and I want to get out!"

I twist and turn slowly,
I stretch my legs wide.
The cocoon cracks open,
and I wriggle outside.

I'm wet and I'm cold
so I turn to the sun.
My wings start to unfold.
I am ready for fun!

In spring I hatched out
from a big mass of eggs.
I munched on green grass,
and I had lots of legs.

But now things have changed.
Now I know how to fly!
I can zig—I can zag.
I can soar through the sky!

I see others fly past.
I watch where they go.
Some of them land on
bright flowers below.

I, too, fly to flowers.
I taste with my feet.
I sip a red blossom—
Oh my, what a treat!

I look at my face
in a small drop of dew.
I'm amazed to see
that I look so brand-new!

A friendly voice says:
"We should go for a ride!"
We soar with the wind.
We fly high and then glide.

We spy some more flowers.
We swirl to them with glee.
In a field full of blossoms
we both go on a spree!

More friends come join us.
We sip sweet, yummy blooms.
"Watch out!" someone cries
as a dark shadow looms.

We all flutter away
just before the attack.
That cat was sure looking
to have us for a snack!

We find a safe place
when the day turns to night.
My friends and I sleep
under leaves, out of sight.

In the morning we wake
and warm our cool wings.
We take to the air
to see what the day brings.

We flap and we flutter,
We zoom in a warm breeze.
We swirl and we tumble,
and zigzag through trees.

We slurp colorful blooms
and sip from a mud puddle.
We rest in cool shade,
all of us in a huddle.

Some of my new friends
lay their eggs in a mass.
Soon babies will hatch,
and munch on the green grass.

A caterpillar will grow
and she'll gaze to the sky.
Like me, soon she'll be . . .

a brand-new butterfly!